ELIJAH'S UNIQUE PERSPECTIVE

CHLOE E. GORE

A Book about Autism for Kids

My name is Elijah and sometimes I feel like I'm different from other kids.

I have autism, which means my brain works a little differently than theirs.

I'm unique in my own way - that's what my mom says!

Cherry! Cherry! Cherry!

I often repeat what I hear, and sometimes I don't even realize I'm doing it.

It's just something my brain needs to do.

Once, while I was in a store, I heard the word 'cherries' and couldn't stop repeating it over and over again - cherries, cherries, cherries - as if I had discovered a new, magical sound that brought me into a state of euphoria and fascination.

I have trouble understanding some situations that may be obvious to other people.

In those situations, when someone tries to hug me or show me emotions in a different way.

I may feel disoriented and uncertain because I'm unable to read the intentions or signals someone is trying to convey to me.

That's when I retreat into my own world.

My head is always filled with countless thoughts, and sometimes it's hard for me to make sense of them.

There are so many thoughts that it's difficult for me to understand what's really going on.

Sometimes they are so chaotic and unstable that it's hard for me to focus on a task or play.

This is particularly frustrating because sometimes I feel lonely and unheard when I can't express my thoughts and feelings.

I don't really like noise and it can sometimes be overwhelming and unpleasant for me.

It's too loud and chaotic for me.

When I hear noise, my head starts spinning and I feel lost.

Some sounds, like a ringing phone or slamming doors, make me anxious.

I often find myself running away or seeking a place where I can calm down.

In such situations, I need help and understanding.

When I do what I love, my body and mind become calm and relaxed.

I enjoy jumping, spinning, and moving my body in different ways.

This helps me to calm down and ease the tension I sometimes feel.

I often do this when I feel anxious or stressed.

Jumping, spinning, or performing other movements allows me to release energy and cope with my emotions.

In this way, I can better understand my feelings and focus on what is important to me.

My behavior may sometimes seem strange or inappropriate to other people.

However, for me, it is a way of coping with difficulties and relaxing.

That is why I need acceptance and understanding from my family and environment.

It is an important part of my life.

I can't express everything with words, so I reach for paper and pencil to transfer my thoughts onto a sheet. When I draw, my hand moves chaotically across the paper, and the shapes and lines that appear on the page are seemingly disorganized and random. For some, it may look like simple scribbles, but for me, it's something more.

It's a way to express myself and my inner world. They are very important to me, and it's a way to reach me. Every shape and line on my paper has its own meaning and significance. When I look at them, I can see the whole story hidden behind them.

For me, drawing is therapy.

I calm down.

When I draw, I feel peaceful and relaxed.

Sometimes beautiful works are created.

And I am proud of them.

Often I feel disoriented and unsure of how to proceed in complex situations.

I need help to identify the source of my anxiety.

Once, while taking a walk, I saw a huge balloon floating in the air.

I wanted to understand the situation, but everything was happening too fast and I couldn't make sense of it. Despite the uncertainty and fear, I stood my ground and didn't give up.

Seeing how everything seemed complicated and chaotic, I was grateful for the support I receive every day from people who understand me and help me understand such situations.

Thanks to them, I feel more confident and hopeful that in the future, I will be able to cope with similar difficulties.

Sometimes I have difficulty controlling my emotions, especially when something doesn't go according to my plan.

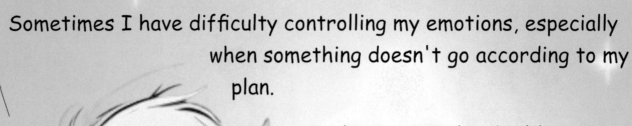

Today I wanted to build a tower out of blocks, but after several attempts, I couldn't keep it standing for more than a few seconds. I started to get frustrated.

My hands started shaking and my eyes were watering.

I yelled and hit the blocks on the floor.

I was very upset that I couldn't do what I wanted to do.

My mom noticed that I was having a problem and tried to calm me down.

She said she knows it's difficult for me, but she's there to help me.

She asked me to try starting over and building the tower again. She explained that only blocks are used on the tower, not the ball that I wanted to place on top.

I calmed down and started over. Unfortunately, I got upset again when the tower fell over.

My mom came over and suggested that we build it together.

I listened to her. The tower was huge. I put the ball aside.

When the tower was finished, I was very happy and smiling.

I also go to therapy, it's like playing with caregivers who help me learn new things and develop my skills.

My caregiver is Andy, she's very funny and I always have a great time with her.

In therapy, I learn how to control my emotions, understand the world around me, play with other kids, and build relationships.

I feel safe there because I know the caregivers are there to help and protect me. Every time I learn something new and I never get bored there.

Therapy is a great place where I can develop my skills and take advantage of new opportunities.

When I had my birthday, I received the most wonderful gift in the world - a puppy! I named him Hau because he loved to bark and jump at me with love. Since that day, I haven't been separated from my friend for a step. I love playing ball with him the most. I throw him the ball, and he always runs after it until he brings it back. It makes me feel happy and full of energy.

But Hau is not just my toy.

When I feel worried, sad, or scared, Hau is with me.

I lie next to him, and he affectionately licks my hand, jumping on me. I feel my body relax and the fear subsides.

He understands me and never judges me.

Thanks to him, I feel really good and safe.

I really don't like getting dressed. I've always had a problem with it. It usually took a very long time and often ended in my frustration. I would scream loudly!

However, Andy - my therapist showed me how I could make this task easier for myself. I slowly mastered this difficult skill.

Now, when I start getting dressed, I always have a set order. This makes me feel less overwhelmed and I don't have to make too many decisions at once.

And when I manage to get dressed, I am always happy and proud of myself. It's a wonderful feeling!

Sometimes I have trouble building relationships with other kids, which makes me feel lonely.

My mind is always full of thoughts that circle in a chaotic way, which makes it hard for me to focus on one thing.

Often, I don't understand what other people are doing, so I watch them from afar instead of participating in games.

My mind works differently than most people, which makes it not easy for me to build relationships.

Sometimes my thoughts and interests are very different from what interests others, which further complicates my communication.

I often feel lonely, and for safety, I simply choose to watch others from a distance, which gives me a sense of participation in games.

I would really like to talk to someone, but sometimes it's hard for me to find the right words to express my thoughts and feelings. That's why I often use gestures and facial expressions to communicate. If you notice that this is how I communicate and make contact with me, I would be happy to play with you.

Even though I have difficulties in establishing relationships with other children, I am trying very hard to develop my social skills. Gradually, I am learning how to build relationships with others and how to function better in a group. Sometimes I need more time and space to understand and accept others, but I believe that I am capable of learning how to communicate with people and establish relationships with them in the best possible way.

I feel a special joy and relaxation when I devote time to activities that bring me pleasure.

Often on sunny days, I sit under a tree in the company of my dog Hau. In such moments, I simply observe the world around me, enjoy the warmth of the sun's rays, and the

closeness of my friend. My love for Hau is immense, and the time spent with him gives me a lot of satisfaction.

For me, it is an important way to relax and unwind, which helps me detach from the stressful reality.

I am convinced that our body knows best what it needs to regenerate after a hard day.

In this way, I learn to enjoy the small things.

I know how important it is to spend time resting. I really need it to function in a healthy way.

I feel incredibly proud when I manage to achieve my goals.

In the past, I was weak at drawing, and my limited hand movements made it difficult for me to create lines and shapes.

I often felt angry that I couldn't express myself and what I feel.

However, instead of giving up, I continued to work and tried to improve my skills.

My loved ones helped me with this by supporting me and encouraging me to keep trying.

One day, I managed to paint a butterfly for the first time, something that was close to my ideal.

I felt an incredible sense of pride in myself because I had managed to overcome my weakness and achieve a goal that had seemed unattainable for a long time.

This moment was very important to me because it made me realize that I couldn't give up in the face of difficulties.

I still try to improve my skills.

When I have too many thoughts in my head, I feel emotionally and physically overwhelmed.

That's when I need a moment to catch my breath and find a way to relax. One of my ways of doing this is to escape into my own world and retreat within myself.

Playing is a way for me to detach from everyday life and unwind. I have my favorite toys that I like to spend time with, and which bring me joy and a sense of security.

When I play with them, I feel free and can focus on the present moment.

Often, when I have too many thoughts, I play a music box or I arrange something.

These activities help me detach from reality and focus on one thing.

This way, I can relax and calm my emotions.

When I am in my own world, I feel free and unrestricted.

I don't have to pretend to be someone I'm not.

I can be myself. This is how I learn to deal with my emotions and stressful situations.

However, this doesn't mean I avoid contact with other people. I simply need time for myself to recharge my batteries and come back to everyday life with new energy.

Playing is a way for me to find emotional balance.

Every day, with every obstacle and every attempt, I learn something new. My thoughts are often chaotic and I struggle to gather them, but with the help of the caring support of my loved ones, I overcome difficulties and develop my skills.

Through determination and hard work, I am building my world boldly and with confidence.

Sometimes I may feel scared or lost, but I know that I can always count on the support of those who love me and care for me.

I have my goals and dreams, which I strive to achieve every day.

I am not afraid to take on challenges, even if they are difficult or require sacrifices. I am aware of my weaknesses, but at the same time, I know that every failure is a lesson that can be used in the future.

I face new challenges, learn something new, and develop my skills.

Backed by the caring support of my loved ones, I am building my world boldly and confidently, step by step achieving my goals and fulfilling my dreams.

Even if I'm different, I'm still myself.

And every day, I learn how to navigate this world and be the best version of myself that I can be.

Each day, I am learning how to be myself and embrace my weaknesses.

With the help of my loved ones, I know that discovering and developing my potential can help me achieve my dreams.

I am not afraid to be who I am!

I realized that my autistic traits are part of me and make me unique.

There is so much diversity in the world, and this is what makes our world beautiful.

Made in the USA
Coppell, TX
11 November 2023

24077468R00019